THIS BOOK BELONGS TO:

ISBN 978-1-7334149-0-6

Published in the United States

Printed in China

BARTHOLOMEW BABBITT'S
BEDTIME BLASTOFF

WRITTEN & ILLUSTRATED BY ANDREW J. HALL

To Bekah, I couldn't do any of this without you!

YOURS -AH

Bartholomew Babbitt had a very bad habit
of playing in bed for hours and hours…

Spread on his bed
was his bear he named Fred,
he monocled walrus with hair on his head,
and a giant gorilla who was actually red.

He'd swing and he'd swoop
and jump up-n-down,

he'd pounce and he'd bounce and run all around.

"Oh, all that noise!" his father said with a grin.

"I'd say an adventure is about to begin!"

Bartholomew's mother laughed with delight,
"Oh! What a fun, adventurous night!"

Now sitting in bed
with eyes wide awake,
his room began to rumble
and tumble and shake!

And there on his bedposts, rockets appeared, wings on the side, and his sheets disappeared!

"BLASTOFF!!"

He squealed
in glorious delight,

and his rocket ship bed soared off into flight,
leaving the world down below and his house out of sight.

Shot into space they flew and they flew,
on past a shuttle, they waved at the crew!
They zipped by the moon and wouldn't ya know?!?
They sped by some aliens in a blue UFO!

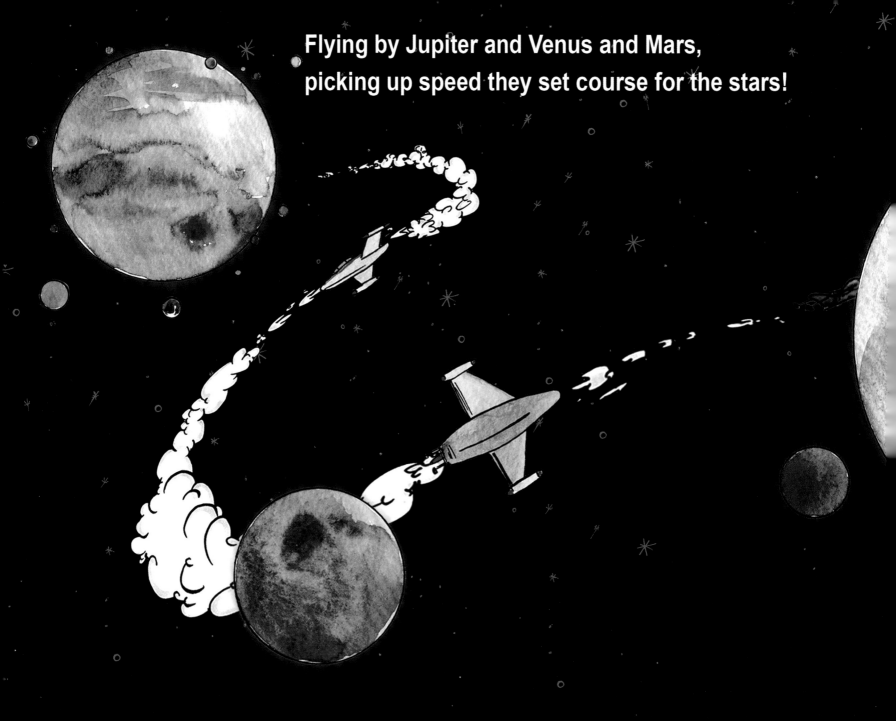

Flying by Jupiter and Venus and Mars,
picking up speed they set course for the stars!

Walrus, he grinned
as they passed the space station.
"Onward!" said Fred,
"to those bright constellations!"

Into the asteroid belt
they zigzagged and veered,
when there in the distance
great beasts did appear!

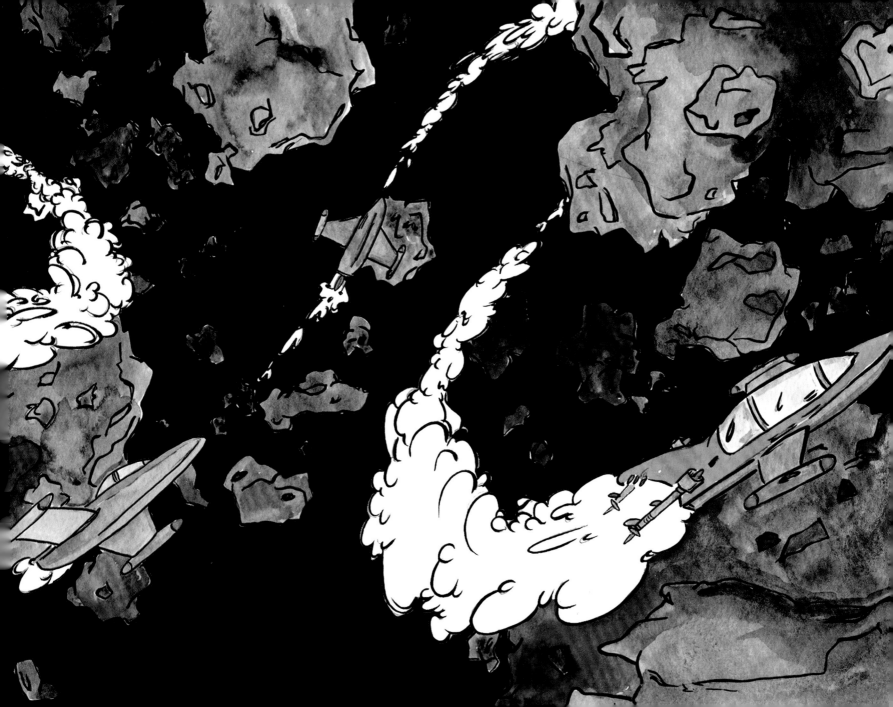

When closer they got, you wouldn't believe,

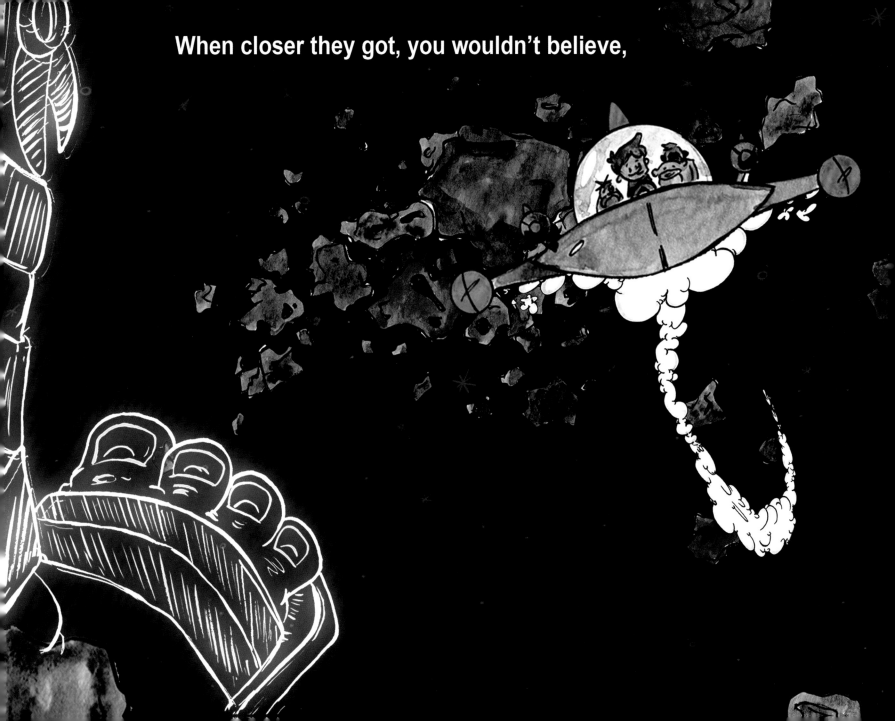

creatures so high, you couldn't conceive!

A lion named Leo and a bear oh so grand,
Orion the hunter with a sword in his hand.
A bull and a crab to the left and the right,
and a scorpion and dog—they all lit up the night!

Everyone waved and said their hello.
The bull gave a snort and the bear a bellow!
Leo, he roared and Orion kneeled down...

...while the scorpion and crab just ran all around.
The dog licked the ship, what a slobbery mess,
and gave a sweet howl in joyful express.

The creatures all smiled as the rocket sped by
and everyone waved to say their goodbye.

On towards the sun, the rocket ship flew,
but boy was it hot for the rocket ship crew!

Bartholomew yawned and gave a big smile.

"It's time we head home, we've been gone for a while!"

"Light speed!!" he said with eager command.
"AYE!" said the gorilla from the helm that he manned.

At lightning-fast speed to earth they did zoom,
then made a soft landing back in their room.

Tucked in cozy with stars overhead,
Bartholomew Babbitt's asleep in his bed.
His parents returned and kissed him good night
while hugging his crew in his arms he held tight

And Bartholomew Babbitt grinned with delight
'cause of the fun in his bed from morning till night.